Vet Barbie

Vet Barbie

A story by
Geneviève Schurer

Illustrations by
Liliane Crismer

HINKLER
BOOKS

First published by Hemma Publications 1997
English edition published by Hinkler Books Pty Ltd 2004
17-23 Redwood Drive
Dingley VIC 3172 Australia
www.hinklerbooks.com

ISBN 1 7412 1776 8
Edited by Juile Haydon
Printed & bound in Australia

Contents

Chapter 1

Welcome to Tourneville

'Are you sure we weren't supposed to take the small road that we just passed?' Barbie asks. 'Dr Martin mentioned an intersection by an oak tree.'

'I am the navigator,' Skipper replies. 'And according to the navigator we'll turn at the stop sign and not before!' Skipper has spent the morning consulting maps and street directories. She has done a fine job of guiding Barbie through the pretty countryside.

'Oh!' Barbie cries suddenly. 'That's your sign up there, the stop sign. And just after that, I can see a big oak. That's the turn-off.'

'The directions that Dr Martin sent us are spot-on. Now, if we turn on to that road and

continue along it, we will reach the village in a few minutes. I told you that with a navigator as talented as me, there was no chance we'd get lost,' Skipper says proudly.

Barbie laughs. She rests her elbow on the open window of

her jeep, and enjoys the feel of the cool breeze against her face. The breeze stirs the leaves on the trees that line the road.

'It's very pretty countryside,' she says, casting her eye over the green meadows. Sheep are dotted over the rolling hills.

A little further along the road, our friends hear the sound of a river. The merry murmuring of the river makes Skipper feel like going for a swim. 'While you're replacing Dr Martin, I'm going to go for a swim every day,' Skipper says mischievously.

'No, that's out of the question,'

Barbie protests. 'You're going to be my assistant. For the next two months, I'll be the only vet for thirty kilometres. We're going to have our work cut out for us!'

'Well, what about Sundays? Would that be okay?' Skipper asks.

'Of course,' Barbie says. 'We'll take time off on Sundays. There'll be picnics, parties and swimming.'

'I can't wait! I'll happily be your assistant during the week, then. Hey, do you think that you can let me be in charge of some kittens? I love kittens.'

'Maybe,' Barbie says, 'though I don't think there will be a lot of time for playing. Look! Here is the village. These are the first houses. Aren't they cute?'

'Dr Martin's house is in a street near the church,' says Skipper, reading their directions. 'I can already hear the bells.'

'Look! There's the church. There's a wedding going on.'

'Oh, Barbie, can we please stop? I love weddings!'

'All right, I'll park the car. Welcome to Tourneville, my lovely assistant.'

There is a large crowd outside

the church. The bells ring as people gather to get a glimpse of the newlyweds. The village has a party atmosphere.

Barbie and Skipper head towards the crowd, and a young man with sparkling eyes gives them a handful of confetti. 'You throw it on the newlyweds. It brings good luck,' he explains.

Suddenly, the doors of the church open wide and the first guests step out of the church. They form a line on either side of the steps to get a good view of the wedding party. The flower girls leave the church. They wear cream dresses. Two little boys wearing light green are next. The children are proud to lead the wedding party.

'Here come the newlyweds! The bride and the groom!' Skipper cries.

The young, smiling woman
who stands on the threshold of
the church is delightful to look
at in her long, white dress. A
veil covers her hair. She holds a
bunch of pretty flowers against

her chest. Her husband stands proudly by her side. Encouraged by the crowd, he kisses his new wife tenderly. At that moment, confetti rains on their heads. As they walk down the steps, they are illuminated by the flash of many cameras. Everyone claps.

'What a lovely way to be introduced to Tourneville,' Barbie says happily to Skipper.

Chapter 2

Dr Martin

Dr Martin's house is surrounded
by a large rose garden. There is
an apple orchard along one side
of the house. Downstairs, there
is a waiting room, an office and

the surgery. Dr Martin lives with his charming wife and two mischievous boys on the first floor.

'Welcome to Tourneville!' says Dr Martin, as he rushes to meet Barbie and Skipper. 'Did you find the house easily?'

'Your directions were perfect. And I also had a splendid navigator,' Barbie says, smiling. 'But the navigator loves weddings, so we lost a little bit of time standing in front of the church.'

'Clementine was getting married. She's the local school-teacher. We are invited to the reception. Clementine told me that I should bring you two along, if you want to. It will be great fun.'

'Wonderful!' Skipper exclaims. 'I love dancing.'

'Emma,' says Dr Martin, as his wife appears, 'this is Barbie

and Skipper. Let's show them to their rooms.'

Barbie and Skipper follow Emma as she leads them to their two pretty bedrooms. They thank Dr Martin's sons, who carry their luggage up the stairs.

'Mum, can we go and ride our bikes?'

'Can we ride to the park?'

'Yes, go,' their mother says, laughing. She turns to her guests. 'They are so excited to be on holidays. Usually, my husband hates to leave his patients, but I think this time he is confident that they'll be in good hands.'

'You can be sure that we'll keep everything in good order,' Barbie says. 'I hope you have a lovely holiday.'

'You'll need to watch out for Cad, Mr Green's little donkey,' Dr Martin says. 'The poor thing had been badly treated when he first arrived here. I think he was depressed.'

Barbie smiles. The two months she will be spending in Tourneville replacing Dr Martin won't be too difficult if her main task is lifting the spirits of a grumpy donkey.

'Do you think you could look

after my roses while I'm away?'
Emma asks shyly.

'I'd love to look after them,'
says Skipper.

'Oh, good. You've made me
feel much better. Now I'd better
leave you with my husband. I'm
going to get ready for the reception. See you soon.'

Dr Martin takes them on a quick tour of the vet clinic. The waiting room is spacious and modern. There are magazines piled up on a table and comfortable seats for the patients. The surgery is well equipped. Barbie knows she will soon feel at home there.

'We're leaving tomorrow,' Dr Martin says. 'Then the house will be all yours. And the animals, too. I hope you enjoy your stay here. Now, let's get ready for the reception.'

Chapter 3

Clementine's reception

To look her best at the reception, Barbie chooses a pretty dress with a pink tulle skirt. It makes her look like a ballerina. Skipper slips into a gorgeous floral dress and ties a white satin ribbon in her hair.

'The wedding reception is going to be held in the courtyard of the local school,' Emma explains, as they drive together to the school. 'Oh, listen! We can already hear the music.'

When they arrive, they see a large buffet table sitting inside a marquee. There is a superb cake in the middle of the table, decorated by two marzipan figures of the newlyweds.

'Dr Martin!' Clementine cries, as she comes over to the little group. 'I'm so happy to see you!'

Clementine has removed the veil from her face, but she still holds the bouquet. Clutching her flowers, Clementine looks like a beautiful fairy.

'Clementine, I wish you all the happiness in the world,' says Dr Martin. 'I'd like to introduce you

to Barbie. She'll be replacing me at the vet clinic while I'm on holiday. And this is her sister, Skipper.'

'Welcome to Tourneville,' Clementine says. 'I'll come and visit you as soon as I return from my honeymoon. We'll be able to get to know each other. I'd love to show you around the area. But now, enjoy yourselves! Dance!'

'Excuse me, Miss,' a young man says timidly to Skipper. 'Will you dance with me?' Skipper smiles and takes his hand.

'That's Fred,' Clementine

says. 'My younger brother. He loves to dance.'

'Well, he chose the right partner then,' Barbie says, smiling.

'Dr Martin, will you dance with the bride?' Clementine asks.

'Oh, no. I'm a very bad dancer.'

'Go on, James. Be brave!' says Emma.

At that moment, the young groom approaches Barbie. He blows Clementine a kiss. 'I understand that you are the new vet in Tourneville, at least, for the summer. I'm Daniel. I've never danced with a vet. Would you like to?'

As they dance, Barbie and Skipper get to know the wedding guests. Every guest, when it's their turn to speak to the newcomers, seems pleased that Barbie will be taking care of the animals in the region.

'My name is Mark,' a charming young man says to Barbie. 'I'm the electrician, but everyone in town calls me Goldfinger because I'm the best handyman around. If there's anything you need fixed, then don't hesitate to call me.

Whether it's a broken-down car, a piano that needs tuning, or a sick tree, I can fix it.'

'Great!' Barbie exclaims. 'I imagine that I will be calling you. Between my work in the surgery and staying in Dr Martin's big house, I'm sure to need a handyman. Thank you for your offer of help, but right now, I'm dying of thirst.'

'Wait here, please,' Mark says, 'I'll get you a drink.'

'Have you already found a knight in shining armour?' Clementine asks, as she takes Barbie's hand. 'You know, everyone in the village is very friendly. You might never want to leave.'

'I'm already feeling that way. Your wedding has given me a great opportunity to get to know everyone. It's been really marvellous! I know I won't be isolated here. Plus, Skipper has come with me to assist at the vet clinic, and Ken, my best friend, has promised he'll join us here as soon has he's finished his latest article.'

'Is your friend a journalist? That's a great job. Daniel and I are looking forward to getting to know you all better.'

'Tell me about your honeymoon! Where are you going?'

'Oh, it's a surprise. Daniel has been keeping it a secret from me. He just told me to pack my swimsuit, so I think we're going to a tropical resort.'

Chapter 4

Finally alone!

On Sunday morning, Emma pre-pares a delicious breakfast. Barbie and Skipper eat with the Martin family under a large apple tree in the orchard. The food is delicious. The vet's two young boys stamp their feet with impatience. They can't wait to leave on their holiday. They've packed all their games in their suitcases, which Dr Martin has already loaded into the car.

After giving lots of friendly advice and warm embraces, the Martin family hit the road.

'Finally, we're alone,' Barbie says. 'I hope we can remember everything Dr Martin said. He didn't stop giving advice!'

'Calm down, sis,' Skipper says. 'It's Sunday. We need to make the most of our time off work.

Let's go for a swim in the river.'

'An excellent idea! I'm going to find my swimsuit and some towels for us.'

A quarter of an hour later, our friends fly down the country roads in their jeep.

'Stop! There! It's perfect,'

Skipper says suddenly, pointing down a little road. 'I can see a clearing ahead, with the river running through it.'

When they arrive at the clearing, the scene is delightful. There are plenty of shady trees, a nice patch of grass to sunbathe on, and the musical rush of the river. The two young women park their jeep and grab their beach bags. They are wearing their swimsuits under their clothes. They hang their clothes on the low branch of a tree. Then they step carefully into the clear, fresh water.

'This is lovely!' Skipper says.

'The water is cool and gentle. I like it!' Barbie says, then she dives into the water.

Suddenly they hear violent barking. An enormous dog bounds towards them.

'Maybe we're on private property,' Skipper whispers.

'Don't make any sudden moves,' Barbie suggests. 'You should never startle a growling dog or show him that you're scared.'

Barbie's calm demeanour quietens the hound down. He stops barking, stands on the river bank and looks at the two swimmers with curiosity.

'Tex! Tex!' a young man's voice suddenly calls out. 'Where are you, you naughty dog?'

'Woof! Woof!' Tex barks.

Between two trees, Mark, the handyman, appears. He gives the two young women a friendly smile. 'Barbie! Is that you? What a surprise! Okay, Tex, you have to stop barking now. Show a bit more respect towards your doctor.'

'Have we wandered on to your property without knowing it?' Barbie asks.

'This clearing belongs to my grandfather,' Mark replies, 'but it's a well-known swimming spot. You chose well! Can I join you in the water? Tex has been dragging me through the trees, and I'm exhausted.'

Soon, the three swimmers are chatting merrily in the water, while Tex chases butterflies on the bank. Finally, Barbie has a chance to relax!

Chapter 5

A horrible day

It's six o'clock on Monday morning. The sun has barely risen. The telephone rings. A horse on Four Springs Farm refuses to leave its stable and seems sick. Can Barbie come at once? Barbie immediately begins to crawl into some jeans and a t-shirt. She grabs her medical kit. She scrawls a note for Skipper telling her where she has gone. She also writes down the tasks she needs Skipper to do during the day.

Four Springs Farm is hard to find, as it is hidden off a small, winding road. When Barbie arrives, she can see that the horse, Tornado, is not happy at all. His owner is quite worried.

'He has a really important race coming up on Sunday. Do

you think he'll be up to it?' he asks anxiously.

'I can't find anything wrong with him,' Barbie says, as she examines the beautiful animal. 'I think he is just tired from all the training. I'll give him an injection and, with the treatment

I prescribe, Tornado should be in fine form by Sunday.'

'Oh, thank you so much, Doctor.'

Barbie leaves the farm and drives back on to the main road. Outside the vet clinic, she has to slow down because a crowd has gathered. In the middle of the crowd, a little boy is crying as he clutches a dark, hairy bundle. Barbie quickly gets out of her car.

'Oh Jimmy! Jimmy!' the little boy cries.

'Let me see the puppy,' Barbie says, as she approaches the child. 'I'm a vet.'

'A car reversed into the dog,' a witness explains, 'and then the car took off.'

Barbie gently takes Jimmy from the little boy's arms. The dog is unconscious. Barbie quickly takes her stethoscope from her kit and puts it in her ears. Finally, she finds the little dog's heartbeat. It is a little fast, but very strong.

'Jimmy will be all right,' she says. 'Don't cry. Let's go into my surgery. Okay?'

Followed by the reassured little boy, Barbie goes into her surgery.

Skipper rushes over to her. 'Barbie!' she cries. 'The waiting room is completely full. It seems as though every cat and dog in the area has fallen ill today. And there are not only cats and dogs waiting for you!'

'Listen, Skipper, don't stress out. Jimmy has been hit by a car.

I'll be attending him first, and then I'll see to the others. Just ask everyone to be patient.'

Barbie gently lies the puppy on her examining table. The little boy dries his tears. He looks at Barbie as though she is a beautiful angel who has fallen from the sky in order to save his little dog.

'What's your name, young man?' Barbie asks, as she examines the dog.

'I'm Tom,' he says. 'This is Jimmy. I love him so much.'

'Your Jimmy's going to be fine. Don't worry. He's had a terrible fright and he's still in shock. I think he has a broken paw, but it will heal.' Barbie sets Jimmy's paw in plaster. Finally, Jimmy opens his eyes and looks at Tom. Tom is so relieved.

'The cast will come off in six weeks,' Barbie says. 'You'll need to keep him quietly at home until then. All right?'

'Oh, yes! Thanks, Miss,' says Tom, forgetting Barbie's name.

'You had a good fright, too, didn't you? I have some lollies in my desk drawer. Do you want some?'

'Oh, yes, please,' Tom says shyly. 'Thank you, Miss.'

Chapter 6

The day isn't over

Skipper settles little Tom under a large tree in the garden, the little dog in his lap. Calm and reassured, Tom waits for his parents to come and pick him up.

Inside, Barbie is dealing with a new patient. It is a sulky goat named Blanche. Blanche is limping. Her owner tries to lead the goat into the surgery. The goat refuses to move out of the waiting room.

'Go on, Blanche, go on!' the goat's owner grumbles. 'Ah, Doctor! I thought that you would never get here. Blanche hates being inside.'

'I'm terribly sorry,' Barbie says, 'but this morning there was an emergency I had to attend to.'

Finally, Blanche is in the surgery, and Barbie can examine

her. 'Tell me what's wrong with Blanche. Has she been limping for long?'

'I don't know,' the man says.

'I'm going to examine her hooves.'

There is a large splinter stuck in one of Blanche's feet. It is infected. The poor goat must be feeling very ill! Barbie gently

removes the splinter from the foot.

'I'm going to give her an injection of antibiotics. You'll have to give her tablets for the next five days. Then she should be fine.'

After poor little Blanche, Barbie sees two dogs, three cats, a guinea pig, and finally a parrot that no longer wants to talk.

In a rare quiet moment, Skipper sticks her head in the surgery. 'Barbie, did you know that it's already three o'clock? You haven't eaten anything!'

'Three o'clock! The time has just flown. Is there anyone left in the waiting room?'

'No one, but Mr Pierce is waiting for you at his farm and Mrs Simon wants you to go over and see her cat.'

'Did she say what was wrong with the cat?'

'She's worried because Missy, that's the cat, hasn't done anything silly today. She's been far too quiet.'

Barbie bursts out laughing. 'It may be nothing then.'

'I've made you a sandwich,' Skipper says. 'Eat it before you leave. Phew! What a busy day we've had today!'

'And the day isn't over yet,' Barbie replies.

Barbie hurriedly eats her lunch, then gets into her jeep. A few minutes later, she arrives at Mr Pierce's farm. She meets the little calf he is hand-rearing. There's still the visit to Mrs Simon's to go, before Barbie can take a break.

Chapter 7

Rescue on the road

When Barbie enters Mrs Simon's lounge room, Missy is lying listlessly in an armchair, a sad expression on her face. Barbie sits down on a chair near the white cat and gently pats her on the head. Missy barely moves. Barbie listens to her heartbeat and finds that it is normal. Then she holds the stethoscope to the cat's ears, so the cat can listen to its own heartbeat. The cat does not react. Barbie is increasingly puzzled.

'Is Missy sick?' asks Mrs Simon, who is quite worried.

'I can't seem to find anything wrong,' Barbie replies.

Barbie lifts one of the cat's paws, and as she does so, an idea comes to her. Slowly, so that the cat understands what she says, she talks to Mrs Simon.

'Missy is very ill,' Barbie says. 'I'll have to give her a rather large injection. It might be a good idea if she stays at the clinic over-night.'

Hearing these words, Missy opens her eyes. She looks at

Barbie, but Barbie's expression is completely serious. All at once, the cat seems to come alive again. She stands up energetically. Turning her back on Mrs Simon and Barbie, she climbs on top of the cupboard and miaows triumphantly.

'Oh, Missy!' sighs Mrs Simon. 'What a little devil you are! This behaviour is impossible!'

'I thought she was playing up, Mrs Simon. That's why I mentioned the large injection. I think your cat is a great little actress.'

'She does boss me around,'

Mrs Simon confesses, 'but if you knew how much fun I have with her. I'm just so sorry to have called you out here for no reason. How can I get her to behave?'

'I'm sure Missy is a lot of fun, but you must reprimand her when she's naughty. Otherwise, one day she will get sick and we won't know if she's acting or not.'

Barbie hits the road again. She is tired but pleased. Her first day of work in Tourneville is over.

The jeep jolts along a small, gravel road. Then suddenly, the car engine hiccups and stops.

'Oh, no!' Barbie says. 'That's all I need: a breakdown. And I'm in the middle of nowhere, too.'

Barbie tries to start the engine, but has no luck. She lifts the bonnet to signal that the car has broken-down. But who will see it? It seems as though there isn't a soul around for miles.

'I don't think anyone will find me,' she says, looking about.

Slowly, night begins to fall. It grows dark. The trees cast scary shadows all around her.

'I can try and walk home,' Barbie says to herself, 'but I might get lost. It's probably best if I stay near the car. Skipper will start looking for me shortly. The jeep will be easier for her to spot.'

Soon, it is completely dark. In the trees, night birds begin to wake. The countryside looks scary. To pass the time, Barbie

hums the choruses of her
favourite songs. Suddenly, she
sees a light glimmering at the end
of the road. She hears an engine.
Barbie can feel her heart beating
in her chest. What should she
do? Should she hide? Or should
she make herself seen in order to

get help? A noisy motorcycle is approaching. In a bold move, she turns on the lights of her jeep. In the light, she sees Mark's worried face coming towards her. She recognises him immediately! Her hero! Barbie sighs with relief. This eventful day is almost over. Soon, she will be able to relax.

Chapter 8

Ken arrives

The rest of the week is a little calmer. There are less accidents and fewer emergencies. On Saturday morning, as she has breakfast with Skipper under an apple tree, a car rolls into the driveway. It's Ken! His article is finally finished and he has come to stay with the young women.

'You seem so well settled!' he says, giving each woman a hug.

'Oh, Ken! We're delighted to

see you,' Barbie says. 'Sit with us. I have some free time before I have to see my first patient.'

'How is your work going?' Ken asks. 'Is the life of a vet very tough?'

Barbie bursts out laughing. 'Well, it's not always easy.' Quickly, she tells Ken about her work in Tourneville.

'What a busy time you're having! It's good that I'm here to help.'

'Oh, don't you know that Barbie has already found a guardian angel?' Skipper teases. 'His name is Mark. He's the one who found Barbie when her car broke down.'

'What a little devil you are, Skipper,' Barbie says, laughing. 'I can't wait to introduce you to Mark, Ken. He's adorable.'

'Well, tomorrow is Sunday,' Skipper says. 'We can all go and swim in the river that cuts through the clearing his grand-father owns.'

'Yes, but for the moment we have to work. So, Skipper, will you show Ken to his room? I'll open the clinic.'

In the afternoon, Barbie takes Ken with her as she goes to

check on her patients. She shows him Cad, the little donkey, who she enjoys cuddling from time to time, to stop him from getting too depressed. Then, she goes to check on Blanche's foot. Finally, she pays a visit to Tom and

Jimmy, who walks around the house quite well despite his plaster.

'You've already done so much good work in this village,' Ken says, as they drive back to the house. 'Well done.'

'Look!' Barbie says suddenly. 'Do you see the little path that goes through those poplar trees? That takes you to Mark's clearing and to our favourite swimming spot. Tomorrow, we'll take a picnic and you'll be able to see how lovely it is.'

'I think that someone else has discovered your little piece of paradise,' Ken says. 'Look. There's a car.'

'What? Who's there?' Barbie asks. 'I liked how deserted it was.'

'Well, you're going to have to share it,' Ken remarks.

'I wonder who they are? Perhaps we can call Mark and see if he knows who the swimmers are.'

When they return to the house, Skipper comes running outside. 'Barbie! Barbie! The farmer from Four Springs Farm called. One of his horses has hurt itself during training. Can you go to the farm now?'

'Okay. It seems that you two will have to have dinner without me,' Barbie says. 'By the time I've gone to the farm, looked after the horse, and driven back, it will be very late. What a pity!'

'I'll come with you,' Ken says. 'There's no question of you

being out alone on these difficult country roads. Imagine if something else happened to the jeep? I'm good with horses, too. Don't wait for us, Skipper. Just leave us some leftovers.'

Chapter 9

A mysterious young woman

On Sunday, the weather is magnificent. There is not even the smallest cloud in the sky. Birds sing from the treetops and the wind carries the scent of roses.

'We've earned our day of rest,' Barbie says, as she steps into the kitchen. 'The river is waiting for us.'

'I've packed us a picnic lunch,' Skipper says.

'I'll put everything into the car,' Ken offers and he picks up the picnic basket.

'The only thing I've got to do today is call up and see if Sultan, the horse, is feeling better,' Barbie says, picking up the phone.

A few minutes later, our friends are driving to the river. They sing happily in the car. As they approach the poplars, Barbie sees the mysterious car once again.

'Well, well, well,' Skipper says. 'Who has invaded our territory?'

'As Ken said yesterday, we'll have to learn to share,' Barbie says. 'After all, the river isn't ours.'

Barbie parks the jeep next to the small black car. The tinted car windows conceal the interior. Sitting on a rock by the water, there is a young woman and an old woman. A little dog frolics about in the water. The women are speaking softly as they dip their feet into the river. When they see our friends, they fall silent. The young woman quickly lowers her eyes. Barbie thinks the girl is very pretty. She has golden skin and big black eyes.

'Hello,' Barbie says, smiling.

Without speaking, the girl bows her head. The old woman

smiles. It is obvious they do not wish to chat, so our friends set up their picnic. When the girl sees Barbie take out the picnic basket, she realises that Barbie and her friends will be staying for a while. The young woman whispers some words into the old woman's ear and together they dry their feet and slip on their sandals. They nod their heads at our friends, then collect their dog and get back into their car. Their car starts up and drives off.

'What a strange girl!' Skipper exclaims. 'She barely responded to us.'

'She seemed very shy,' Barbie remarks.

'Or maybe she just wanted to keep to herself,' Ken adds.

'I think we disturbed them. Perhaps they wanted to enjoy the isolation of this place,' Barbie says.

'Have you seen them before in the village, Barbie?' Ken asks.

'No, no. Never.'

'I've seen the car before,' Skipper says. 'Outside the bakery.'

'If they have been shopping for food, then maybe they are staying in the village,' Ken says.

'It's all very mysterious,' Skipper says, smiling. 'I love mysteries.'

Chapter 10

The mystery thickens

After a quick swim in the fresh water, Barbie opens the picnic basket. Starving, our friends devour the delicious salads and rolls that Skipper has prepared.

Then Mark arrives with his dog, Tex. He is just in time. Ken was about to eat the last slice of cake! The two men introduce themselves and quickly become firm friends. After lunch, everyone lies in the sun. The conversation turns to the encounter with the mysterious girl. Barbie asks Mark if he knows who she is.

'I know exactly who you're talking about,' Mark says. 'The girl, the old woman and the little dog arrived here a few days ago. They rented a house on Brison Road. But they don't speak to anybody. When they go to the village, the girl hangs back while the old woman does the grocery shopping. I've seen them a couple of times by the river. But they stop speaking as soon as I approach them. They only respond to my greeting by nodding their heads.'

'Maybe they speak another language,' Barbie suggests.

'The old woman speaks with a foreign accent,' Mark replies, 'but no one has ever heard the girl speak.'

'Maybe she's hiding from the law,' Skipper says. She loves detective stories.

Barbie bursts out laughing. 'No, I think she might be an actress who's trying to be anonymous.'

'Or perhaps they are refugees,' Ken adds.

'I think you all have great imaginations,' Mark says, with a smile. 'City people often come to the village for some peace and quiet. Maybe that's why the girl is here. I must admit I'm curious about her, too.'

'Ah, you see!' Skipper exclaims. 'I told you it was a mystery. I bet there's a great story here somewhere.'

Our friends decide to play some ball games. They have so much fun that they forget all about the mysterious girl. Later, the men play with Tex, while Barbie and Skipper gather a giant bouquet of daisies from the meadow. They enjoy this Sunday very much. When night falls, our friends feel a little sad. It's a pity that such a wonderful day has to end.

The working week begins again. Barbie is kept busy caring for many sick and injured animals. On Wednesday, chance decides to link our friends with the mystery girl.

At around five o'clock, Barbie and Ken are driving back to the clinic after having visited Mr Green's farm. Ken has turned on the radio. He taps his leg in time to the music.

Barbie suddenly cries out, 'Ken! Look! It's that girl. Gracious! Her dress is covered in blood.'

The girl's steps are heavy as she walks along the side of the road. Against her chest, she holds a ball of dark fluff. As they reach her, Barbie stops the jeep. 'Do you need help?' Barbie calls out. 'Are you hurt?'

'No, no, I'm fine,' the girl says in a voice thick with tears. She is almost choking on her tears. 'It's Zimba, my dog. I think he's going to die.'

Barbie and Ken get out of the jeep. 'Whose blood is that on your dress?' Barbie asks.

'It's Zimba's. He has a big gash behind his ear and he can't move.' Tears are running down the girl's face.

'Come and sit for a moment,' Ken says gently. He points to a large log by the side of the road.

'Leave me with Zimba,' Barbie says, taking the dog from the girl's arms. 'I'm a vet. I can help. Ken, can you get my medical kit from the back of the car?'

Chapter 11

A foreign language

Ken comes back with a blanket and Barbie's medical kit. He helps the girl to sit on the log. The girl cries as though her heart is breaking. She has eyes only for

Zimba. She loves her little dog, but she is afraid that Zimba is dying.

'Tell me what happened,' Barbie says.

'It was a horse,' the girl replies.

'A horse? I don't understand,' Barbie says.

'The horse kicked Zimba. I think the horse was afraid of Zimba.'

'I see,' Barbie says. 'Your dog must have climbed through the fence on to Mr Green's farm. He keeps several horses in the back paddocks. And horses can be quite nervous animals. If your dog approached a horse from behind, the horse may have been startled. It probably kicked Zimba. How frightening for you! Horses are very strong.'

As they talk, Barbie takes care of the little dog. She gives him an injection to help his heart, applies pressure to the cut to stop

the bleeding and examines his head carefully to check for any other wounds.

'I am comfortable around horses,' the girl says. 'My father owns many horses. Tell me, Miss, is Zimba still alive?'

'He's still alive. Don't cry any more. I think that he'll recover, but this is quite a serious injury. He'll need to recover at my clinic,' Barbie says.

'We can take him there now,' Ken says. 'Come with us.'

As soon as she learns that her dog will live, the girl stops crying. Her eyes light up and look as

bright as the sky after a storm.
Ken gets into the back of the jeep
with the dog. Barbie and the girl
sit in the front.

When they arrive back at Dr
Martin's, Skipper immediately
notices their grave faces. Her
eyes open wide when she notices
the mysterious girl.

'Can you get the girl a drink,
Skipper?' Barbie asks. 'I've got
to take care of the little dog.'

A quarter of an hour later,
Barbie reappears in the waiting
room with Zimba in her arms. The
small dog has a bandage on his
head. He looks like a funny egg.

When she sees her little dog, the girl jumps up and runs over to him. Skipper is nowhere to be seen.

'There we go!' Barbie says. 'Zimba has had seven stitches. That's quite a lot, but it could've been worse. He has no broken bones. He's just in a bit of shock.

I'd like to keep him here over-
night for observation.'

When she sees the sad expression on the girl's face, Barbie
can't help adding, 'You can stay
here, too, if you want. Then
there'll be four of us here with
Zimba.'

'Is that true! I can? Oh, thank

you, Doctor. I was worried about being so far away from him. Would it be all right if I use your telephone? I have to call my nana,' the girl says timidly.

'Of course,' Barbie says. 'The telephone's in my office. I'm going to help Skipper make dinner. I hope you're hungry because my sister is a great cook.'

'You are very kind. Thank you.'

Barbie gently closes the office door to give the girl some privacy. Then she goes off to find Skipper, but she's not in the kitchen.

A few minutes later, Skipper walks into the kitchen.

'Where have you been?' Barbie asks.

'Quiet! I was listening to the girl on the phone,' Skipper replies.

'What? Were you eavesdropping?' Barbie asks, shocked.

'No, I was walking past the window of your office when I heard a strange conversation.'

'What was the conversation?'

'Well, I don't know,' Skipper admits. 'The girl was speaking a language I've never heard before. I didn't understand a single word.'

Chapter 12

A lovely name

Curled up on a chair in the lounge room, Zimba sleeps. His head is covered with the enormous bandage, and he breathes faintly, but regularly. The young girl never takes her eyes off him, but all the same, she seems a lot calmer.

Barbie suggests that she change out of her bloodied dress. After she has a shower, Barbie lends her a dress.

A little while later, the girl walks into the kitchen. 'We're the

same size,' she says to Barbie, with a sweet smile.

'We're probably about the same age, too,' Barbie says.

Ken and Skipper are seated at the table with Barbie. They fall silent, waiting for the girl to tell them something about herself, but she says nothing more. The girl obviously doesn't like talking about herself.

'Your family are not too worried, I hope,' Skipper says.

'Oh, perhaps I should call them again. My nana might be worried. She might think I've been kidnapped.'

'Oh, I don't think so,' Ken says, laughing. 'Everyone in this village is lovely.'

'I know,' the girl says, with a sad sigh, 'but I've always had to be very careful.'

'I don't understand,' Barbie says. 'Why?' Ken and Skipper are just as puzzled.

'My father has always protected me,' the young girl says, after a long silence. 'I'm his only daughter, and I'm very important to him. He is a wealthy man and he has always been wary of enemies. I think he has passed on that fear to me.'

'Enemies? What sort of enemies? What does your father do?' Barbie asks.

'It's a little difficult to explain,' the girl says, hesitating.

'Sorry, we don't mean to pry,' Barbie says gently. 'If you don't want to speak about such things, we'll stop asking you questions.'

'I'm sorry,' the girl says. 'I don't mean to be unfriendly. I've always been told not to give out any details of my life. I wouldn't even know where to begin. Perhaps we can talk about this again later.'

'Okay,' Barbie agrees. 'Now, let's talk about Zimba. How old is he?'

'He's just turned four and we've never been apart. He is the only one I can talk to freely. Every night, I tell him all my thoughts. He is my confidant.'

'We saw you the other day with your nana by the river. You

seemed to be enjoying your-selves,' Skipper says.

'My nana came to look after me when my mother died. I love her very much, but I can't tell her what I'm thinking,' the young girl admits.

'Do you think you can tell us your name?' Skipper asks sud-denly. 'We need to know what to call you.'

'Of course! I'm sorry I didn't tell you it before. My name is Selima.'

'Selima! What a beautiful name! It suits you,' Skipper exclaims.

'Selima, that is a beautiful name,' Barbie says. 'Well, welcome, Selima!'

'Thank you! Thank you for everything! It must be wonderful to have friends like you,' Selima says.

'But we are your friends,' Barbie tells her. 'You can count on us. Don't forget that.'

'No, I won't forget. I couldn't forget any of you. You can be sure of that,' Selima says. 'I've had so few friends in my life.'

'Well, because of one little injury, you've made three friends at once!' Barbie says.

Selima bursts out laughing. It is the first time they have heard her laugh!

Chapter 13

A stressful night

Selima wants to sleep in the lounge room to be close to Zimba. Barbie sets her up with blankets and a pillow on the couch facing Zimba's bed.

'Don't hesitate to call me if Zimba wakes up and seems agitated,' Barbie says.

'I hope I won't have to bother you,' Selima replies. Zimba is sleeping calmly.

Several hours later, Barbie is dreaming that she has won an equestrian competition with Tornado, when she hears a knock on her door. She comes completely awake. She puts on her dressing gown and opens the door.

In the doorway, wearing a loose t-shirt, is Selima. She seems very worried. 'I think

Zimba is getting worse. He's having a fit. It's awful!'

'Let's go!' Barbie says.

'I hope we don't wake the others,' Selima says.

The rest of the house is completely silent. 'Skipper and Ken are heavy sleepers,' Barbie says.

On his couch, Zimba seems very unsettled. He trembles all over and chatters his teeth.

Barbie grabs her medical kit from the clinic and examines the little dog. 'He has a slight temperature,' she says. 'It's not too bad. I've already given him some antibiotics. Zimba!' Barbie says gently, as she pats the little dog. 'Wake up, little one! I think that his tremors are just a result of the shock he had today.'

Slowly, the little dog opens his eyes and stops trembling.

'You were having a nightmare,
that's all, poor little Zimba,'
Selima says. 'I think that the big
black horse will haunt your
dreams for a little while longer,
but you have to forget him.'

'I'll give him a little bit of water to drink, but don't worry, Selima, he'll be all right. In a few days, he'll be up and about. I just hope that he's learnt his lesson and stays away from horses,' Barbie says.

'I hope so, too. Otherwise he'll be in trouble at my father's.'

'Does he have many horses?'

'About twenty of them,' Selima answers. 'It's a stable for racehorses. He's very proud of his horses. He takes great care of them. The stables are carefully monitored and air-conditioned, and my father built the horses a pool, so that they can swim and develop their muscles.'

'Air-conditioned stables!' Barbie bursts out. Selima's father must be very wealthy if he can treat his horses so luxuriously.

Barely illuminated by the lamp, facing Barbie, Selima seems to gain more confidence. Night is always when people feel like sharing secrets and Barbie is a very attentive friend.

'Does your father have air-conditioned stables because you live in a hot country?' Barbie asks.

'Absolutely,' Selima says. 'There is a desert everywhere,

broken only by oil fields. I live in Arabia.'

'You are a long way from home then!' Barbie exclaims. 'Are you on holiday?'

'If you don't mind, I'd like you to keep this a secret. We're

taking a break, my nana and I,'
Selima explains. 'I came here to
study, but we always have to
live with bodyguards. One day,
Nana and I slipped out of the
house. We got into my car and
decided to take a little holiday
on our own.'

'But your father must be very
worried,' Barbie says.

'I telephoned him as soon as
we arrived in Tourneville. He
understands the reason why I
had to escape for awhile and he
trusts me. He knows that I am
very careful. I told him that
we were staying in a peaceful,

little village and that it is quite safe. Nana and I are having a wonderful holiday. And now I've had the chance to meet you! It's so nice to have a friend.'

Chapter 14

Selima leaves

Barbie and Selima talk for a long time that night, as they watch over Zimba. In the morning, when she goes to the kitchen to make breakfast, Skipper finds the two young women asleep on the couch. Zimba, however, is awake and sniffing around for something to eat.

A few hours later, Selima's nana comes to see her. She has brought some food for Barbie, Ken and Skipper. It is food from her country. Our friends are delighted by the gift of couscous and meatballs.

Selima has admitted that her father is wealthy, but she has not said who he is.

'Maybe he is someone famous,' Skipper suggests.

'In any case, we can't ask her

any more questions,' Barbie says.
'She told me that she is leaving
Tourneville tomorrow. I enjoy her
company, but I think she misses
her home. She must miss her
family and friends and her
horses.'

That evening, our friends have company for dinner. They are joined by Clementine and Daniel, who are back from their honeymoon, and Mark, as well as Selima and her nana. They eat together under an apple tree in the orchard.

'I have had such a wonderful holiday,' Selima says.

'Your beautiful holiday is not over yet,' Skipper protests.

'Oh, it is,' Selima replies. 'My father has asked me to return home, but I'll be back in this country for the start of my classes. I hope we can see each other again.'

'Of course!' Barbie exclaims. 'When you become friends, it's forever.'

'You can always come back to Tourneville,' Clementine says. 'There's plenty of room at our house and you will always be safe with your friends.'

'How can I ever thank you?' Selima replies, with tears in her eyes.

'That's easy, by coming back soon!' Mark says.

The next morning, the little black car drives through the village. All the windows are open and everyone waves goodbye to the women. They drive on to the main road, and start for the city.

'Goodbye, Selima,' Barbie whis-pers, as the car drives off.

Chapter 15

Life continues

Missy has disappeared! Mrs Simon sounds awful on the telephone. She is very upset. Yesterday, she scolded her cat because she tore the curtains in the lounge room. Then, the animal vanished.

'I turned the house inside out,' Mrs Simon moans to Barbie. 'I'm afraid that something has happened to her.'

'We'll be over as soon as we can, Mrs Simon,' Barbie reassures her. 'Missy can't be too far. Your cat's very clever. She wouldn't take stupid risks.'

An hour later, after having taken care of a bird that had fallen from its nest and been rescued by a child, Barbie, accompanied by Ken and Skipper, leaves for Mrs Simon's.

The shredded curtains in the lounge room are evidence of the animal's mischief.

'Gosh! This cat is so spoilt,' Skipper whispers into Barbie's ear.

'Hush! The cat is like Mrs Simon's baby. We've got to find her.'

'Why don't we split up,' Ken suggests. 'I'll take the attic. Skipper, you search the first floor, and, Barbie, you take the ground floor. We'll search the garden together.'

Our friends begin to look under armchairs and coffee

tables, and in cupboards and pantries. They call Missy's name as they search.

Mrs Simon is a wreck. She trots from one searcher to another, asking, 'Have you found her yet? Have you found her yet?'

'She's not in the house, that's for sure,' Ken says, when they've com-pleted their search of the house. 'We've looked every-where. Now it's time to search the garden.'

There are plenty of places for a cat to hide in the garden. Ken and Skipper look in the garden beds, and Barbie walks towards a large oak tree. She looks up into the high branches and hears a soft miaow.

'Here!' Barbie yells. 'I've found her!' Barbie starts to climb the tree.

As Ken and Skipper rush

over, Barbie takes Missy down from a high branch. The little cat is trembling and traumatised.

'What happened?' Ken asks, as Barbie climbs down with the cat in one arm.

'She got stuck on a high branch in the oak tree,' Barbie says. 'I think she was playing hide and seek with us. Look, there's a wound on her back leg. Maybe she was scratched by a possum that she disturbed. I hope that will teach her. Next time, Missy, you'll have to stay near the house.'

'Oh, Missy, my little baby,' Mrs Simon says. 'Who hurt you?

Good gracious, you're bleeding!
Do something, Doctor!'

'I'll put a bandage on that cut,
but you'll have to discipline her in
future. She was hiding from us on
purpose. She is a naughty cat.'

'I think this experience will teach Missy to behave,' Skipper says. 'I don't think she'll want to climb the oak tree again.'

Barbie does as much as she can for Missy, then she leaves the cat with her doting owner.

That evening, Clementine and Daniel drop in for a drink. Barbie tells them about Missy's behaviour.

'You've got to look after children better than that, don't you think, Daniel?' Clementine says.

'I know Mrs Simon a little,' Daniel says. 'All her children have grown up. They've all moved away and rarely come back to see her. So she spoils Missy.'

'Selima would've found this story very amusing,' Barbie says.

'I'm sure there aren't many

cats in Arabia,' Skipper says. 'Not that she told us much about her home.'

'That young girl was so secretive!' agrees Ken. 'But so adorable! We miss her a lot!'

It's true that since Selima left, no one has been able to forget the beautiful girl with the golden skin.

Chapter 16

The black limousine

Barbie's time at the vet clinic is almost at an end. In a few days, Dr Martin will return with his little family. Barbie is very proud to be handing back such a well-organised clinic. She hasn't had any complaints in her two months of working there. All the animals that she has been looking after are now in good health. Dr Martin will be happy.

Ken, who has loved his time in the country, feels very relaxed. He and Mark have become insepara-ble friends. Even though she is sad to be leaving her new friends, Barbie knows that she will come back to visit Tourneville. She wants to see Clementine, Daniel, Mark and even the devilish Missy again.

'So, Tom, how is little Jimmy

going?' Barbie asks, as Tom and Jimmy walk into the surgery. 'He seems to have already forgotten his accident.'

'Yes, but I haven't forgotten it! I was so scared!'

'It was an accident, Tom. It's unlikely that it will ever happen again. Try not to think about it too much. So, why have you come to see me today?'

'It's time for Jimmy's vaccination,' Tom says.

Just as Barbie finishes giving brave Jimmy his injection, she hears the sound of a car engine outside.

A few seconds later, Skipper sticks her head in the door. 'Barbie! Barbie! Have a look! I've never seen such a car!'

Barbie pushes the curtain aside so she can see out the window. A large limousine has parked near the garden. The limousine is so big that an entire

school class could fit behind its many tinted windows.

'What is it doing outside our house?' Skipper asks.

At that moment, Ken, Mark, Clementine and Daniel wheel their bikes up the driveway.

They've been fishing. They put their bikes down near the limousine. They have stunned looks on their faces. Barbie rushes out to meet them.

A car door opens. A man gets out of the car. He wears a long white tunic, buttoned high at the neck, and white trousers. His eyes are hidden behind sunglasses and his head is covered by a white scarf. In the little Tourneville street, the sight is striking!

'Miss Barbie?' asks the man. His accent is foreign.

'Yes, that's me,' Barbie says, as she moves towards him.

'My name is Feizha. I work for the Prince of Oman.'

'But I don't know the Prince of Oman,' Barbie says.

'I think that you know his daughter, Princess Selima.'

'Selima! A princess!' Barbie, Ken and Skipper cry together in surprise.

'The princess had a holiday in this village,' Feizha adds. 'She said that it was the best holiday she'd ever had and that she didn't want to be separated from the friends that she'd made. She asked me to give you these plane tickets so you'll be able to visit her in her palace. She also said to tell you that Zimba is looking forward to seeing you again, and that her father's horses can't wait to meet you.'

For a moment, Barbie can't find her voice. When she finally speaks, she asks, 'Go to her

palace? In Arabia?'

'There's a note with the tickets. I have six tickets to give you. Here they are.' Feizha hands the tickets to Barbie.

Each ticket is in an envelope. Barbie, Ken, Skipper, Mark, Clementine and Daniel are written on the envelopes. There is also a short note in Barbie's envelope. It reads: Come, my friends. Our holiday is not over yet! Selima.

'We're going to see Selima's palace? Yippee!' Skipper cries.

'What a wonderful idea!' Barbie says. 'We will have so much fun!'

The end

Other titles in this series: